AUNT ISABEL
MAKES TROUBLE

KATE DUKE

PUFFIN BOOKS

PUFFIN BOOKS
Published by the Penguin Group
Penguin Putnam Books for Young Readers, 345 Hudson Street, New York, New York 10014, U.S.A.
Penguin Books Ltd, 27 Wrights Lane, London W8 5TZ, England
Penguin Books Australia Ltd, Ringwood, Victoria, Australia
Penguin Books Canada Ltd, 10 Alcorn Avenue, Toronto, Ontario, Canada M4V 3B2
Penguin Books (N.Z.) Ltd, 182-190 Wairau Road, Auckland 10, New Zealand

Penguin Books Ltd, Registered Offices: Harmondsworth, Middlesex, England

First published in the United States of America by Dutton Children's Books, a division of Penguin Books USA Inc., 1996
Published by Puffin Books, a member of Penguin Putnam Books for Young Readers, 1999

1 3 5 7 9 10 8 6 4 2

THE LIBRARY OF CONGRESS HAS CATALOGED THE DUTTON EDITION AS FOLLOWS:
Duke, Kate.
Aunt Isabel makes trouble/by Kate Duke
[author and illustrator].—1st ed.
p.   cm.
Summary: Aunt Isabel tells Penelope the story of Lady Nell, star of the East Woods
nutball team, who pitched ninety-mile-an-hour cherry drops at thieves.
ISBN 0-525-45496-9 (hc.)
[1. Mice—Fiction. 2. Aunts—Fiction.
3. Storytelling—Fiction.]
I. Title.
PZ7.D886Ar 1996 [E]—dc20 95-45813 CIP AC

Puffin ISBN 0-14-056255-9

Printed in the United States of America

For Sidney,
who cheers me up and cheers me on

Penelope and Aunt Isabel had been out all day in the park. "Time to go home," said Aunt Isabel.

"But I don't want to," said Penelope.

"Time for a rest," Aunt Isabel said.

"But I'm not tired," Penelope answered.

"Time to listen to a story," Aunt Isabel continued.

"But—" squeaked Penelope.

"But, but, but!" exclaimed Aunt Isabel. "You make a lot of trouble with all those *buts*."

"But I don't want to just listen to a story," Penelope said. "I want to help tell it."

"Okay," said Aunt Isabel. "We'll tell it together, then. I'll start and you'll keep but-but-butting in. That way we'll make a lot of trouble for this story, and keep it full of surprises. Now, whom shall our story be about?"

"A mouse," said Penelope, "named Penelope."

"Lady Penelope, Nell for short," continued Aunt Isabel, "who travels far and wide, searching for adventure. She's had an exciting summer as star pitcher for the East Woods nutball team. Her team has won every game, thanks to Lady Nell's ninety-mile-an-hour fastball. Now the nutball season is over, though, and Lady Nell can relax and practice her violin and rest."

"BUT SHE'S NOT TIRED!" squeaked Penelope.

BUT-

"You're right," agreed Aunt Isabel. "And besides, the word is out that Cocky the Roach and his gang are on the loose, roaming the countryside and robbing everyone in sight."

"That's trouble!" cried Penelope.

"Indeed it is," said Aunt Isabel. "It's not a good time to be out alone in the woods. So Lady Nell decides to visit her true love, the kind and handsome Prince Augustus, in his nice, safe castle.

"There!" said Aunt Isabel. "No more trouble!"

"BUT—" said Penelope.

"BUT," Aunt Isabel resumed, "when she looks at her calendar to plan her trip, she gets a terrible surprise— today is Prince Augustus's birthday! And she's been so busy playing nutball, she forgot it. 'Drat,' she says. 'If I don't hurry, I'll miss his party. Oh, how sad he'll be!'"

"Yikes," said Penelope. "Trouble again!"

"It's a long, long way to the castle, too," Aunt Isabel added. "How will she ever get there in time?

"'No problem,' thinks Nell. 'I'll fly!'"

"BUT—" said Penelope.

BUT—

"BUT," said Aunt Isabel, "mice can't fly—not without money for a ticket. And Lady Nell has none. She has always been a mouse who would rather have fun and adventures than a penny in her pocket. 'Double drat,' she says. 'I'll just have to walk and hope for the best.'

"And she starts off down the road as fast as she can, fiddling a tune to keep up her spirits. Before long, she comes to a village. 'Aha!' she thinks. 'Someone here is sure to know a shortcut to the castle.'"

"BUT—" said Penelope.

"BUT," Aunt Isabel went on, "she can't find anyone to help her. The streets are empty. What's worse, as she looks into the store windows, she realizes that she hasn't got a present for Augustus—nothing at all."

"Uh-oh!" gasped Penelope.

"And hunt though she may," sighed Aunt Isabel, "she can't find so much as a dime with which to buy a present.

"And she does so want to give Augustus something wonderful...something he's never had before, something big and fun and fast, something in his favorite color—red. What's she going to do?

"'Well,' she says, 'if money's what I must have, I'll just find a way to get some.'"

"BUT—" said Penelope.

"BUT," said Aunt Isabel, "how will she do it in this quiet little village with nobody around? 'No problem,' says Nell.

"And putting her nutball cap on the ground beside her, she starts to play her violin and sing. 'Soon,' she thinks, 'the villagers will come to dance and clap and throw coins into my cap.'"

"BUT—" said Penelope.

"BUT," said Aunt Isabel, "no one comes to dance. No one even listens, except one old mouse who whispers through his door, 'Everyone is hiding from Cocky the Roach and his gang. They've robbed us and raided us and rampaged through the town till we've almost nothing left!' And, indeed, all he has to give Lady Nell are some cherry drops and a pack of gum.

"'Triple drat!' says Nell to herself. With a sigh, she sits down on a bench outside Frank's Sandwich Shop to chew her gum and think of another plan."

"BUT—" said Penelope.

"BUT," cried Aunt Isabel, "something funny is going on! The Sandwich Shop is swarming with enormous bugs!

"'It's Cocky the Roach and his gang!' Nell gasps, almost swallowing her gum. Poor Frank is being robbed!

"'Cash! Cash! Give us all your cash!' she hears the bandits chant. 'Or we'll eat up all your sandwiches! We'll chew your cold cuts! Chomp your cheese! We'll cluster on your lettuce leaves!'

"'No! No!' sobs Frank. He empties the cash register into Cocky's sack.

"'What a cinch!' snickers Cocky. 'Let's scram!'

"The robbers scurry toward the door. It looks like they're going to get away—"

"BUT—" shouted Penelope.

BUT—

"BUT," cried Aunt Isabel, "Nell has a surprise in store. She pulls out her nutball mitt as Cocky runs out. And—ZING! A ninety-mile-an-hour cherry drop, pitched by Lady Nell, star of the East Woods nutball team, whangs him across the kneecaps and whirls him into the air.

"'Crumbs!' he screeches. 'What was that?'"

"ZING! Another crooked cockroach hits the ground.
"ZING! ZING! ZING! The cherry drops keep coming."
"Now *they're* in trouble!" cried Penelope.
"Big trouble!" agreed Aunt Isabel.

"In an instant they're all sprawled on the ground in a tangle of legs and antennae. And before they can so much as twitch, Nell sticks them all together with gum into a big gooey lump.

"'You've saved my store!' shouts Frank.

"'You've saved our town!' cheer the villagers, coming out at last from their hiding places.

"'You're a hero!' cries the Mayor.

"'Glad to help,' answers Nell.

"'We must have a parade,' the Mayor proclaims, 'with you as the star!'

"'A parade!' shout the villagers. 'Hip hip hooray!'"

"BUT—" said Penelope.

"BUT," said Aunt Isabel, "what about Augustus's party? Nell doesn't care about being in a parade. She doesn't care about the sandpiper band or the tumbling toads or the balloons like enormous cherry drops. She doesn't care that she gets to ride in a basket hitched to the biggest balloon, with a

fat cushion to sit on. All she can think about is poor Augustus's birthday.
'If I run very, very fast when this is over,' she thinks, 'I might still get to the
castle in time.'"

"BUT—" Penelope said.

"BUT—" said Aunt Isabel, "then the Mayor makes a speech. It goes on and on. 'Now I'll miss Augustus's birthday for sure,' groans Nell."

"And Augustus will be sad," said Penelope.

"Maybe not," said Aunt Isabel, "because just then the Mayor says, 'And now for your reward!' He unties a string at one corner of Nell's cushion, and out pours—guess what?"

"MONEY!" squeaked Penelope.

"What a wonderful surprise!" exclaimed Aunt Isabel. "It's loot from Cocky the Roach's hideout. There's enough to buy presents for *all* of Augustus's birthdays, and enough for Nell to fly to the castle whenever she wants, forevermore."

"Hooray!" shouted Penelope. "Her troubles are over!"

"BUT—" said Aunt Isabel.

"Hey!" cried Penelope. "Not *more* trouble! I like this ending!"

BUT—!

"BUT," continued Aunt Isabel, "just then the wind blows, Nell's balloon tugs on its strings, and Nell has an idea for another surprise. 'Thanks,' she says to the Mayor, 'but who needs money?' Then she picks up the cushion and empties the whole thing into the air! The crowd gasps and cheers and runs to catch the money as it floats on the breeze."

"This is *terrible!*" wailed Penelope. "A terrible surprise."

"Really?" asked Aunt Isabel. "The villagers don't think so. Nell is more of a hero than ever. And then—the balloon tugs again on her basket. The heavy sack of loot is gone. The basket is light. And Lady Nell weighs hardly anything. The wind blows harder…

"…and Nell's balloon rises swiftly into the sky, sailing higher and higher
and farther and faster, until it comes to rest beside a certain castle."

"Augustus's castle!" squeaked Penelope.

"Exactly," said Aunt Isabel. "And that, my dear Penelope, is how Lady Nell flies to the side of her true love and brings him a large, exciting, fast, fun present in his favorite color—red—just in time for his birthday party. And she does it all without having so much as a penny in her pocket."

"I like that ending," said Penelope. "It had the best surprise."

"And the best present," agreed Aunt Isabel.

"Where does Augustus fly in his birthday balloon?" asked Penelope.

"He and Lady Nell go to Frank's Sandwich Shop a lot," Aunt Isabel replied. "Augustus is very fond of sandwiches."

"Where else?" demanded Penelope.

"That's another story," replied Aunt Isabel.

"But—" began Penelope.

"Shh," whispered Aunt Isabel. "No more *buts!*"